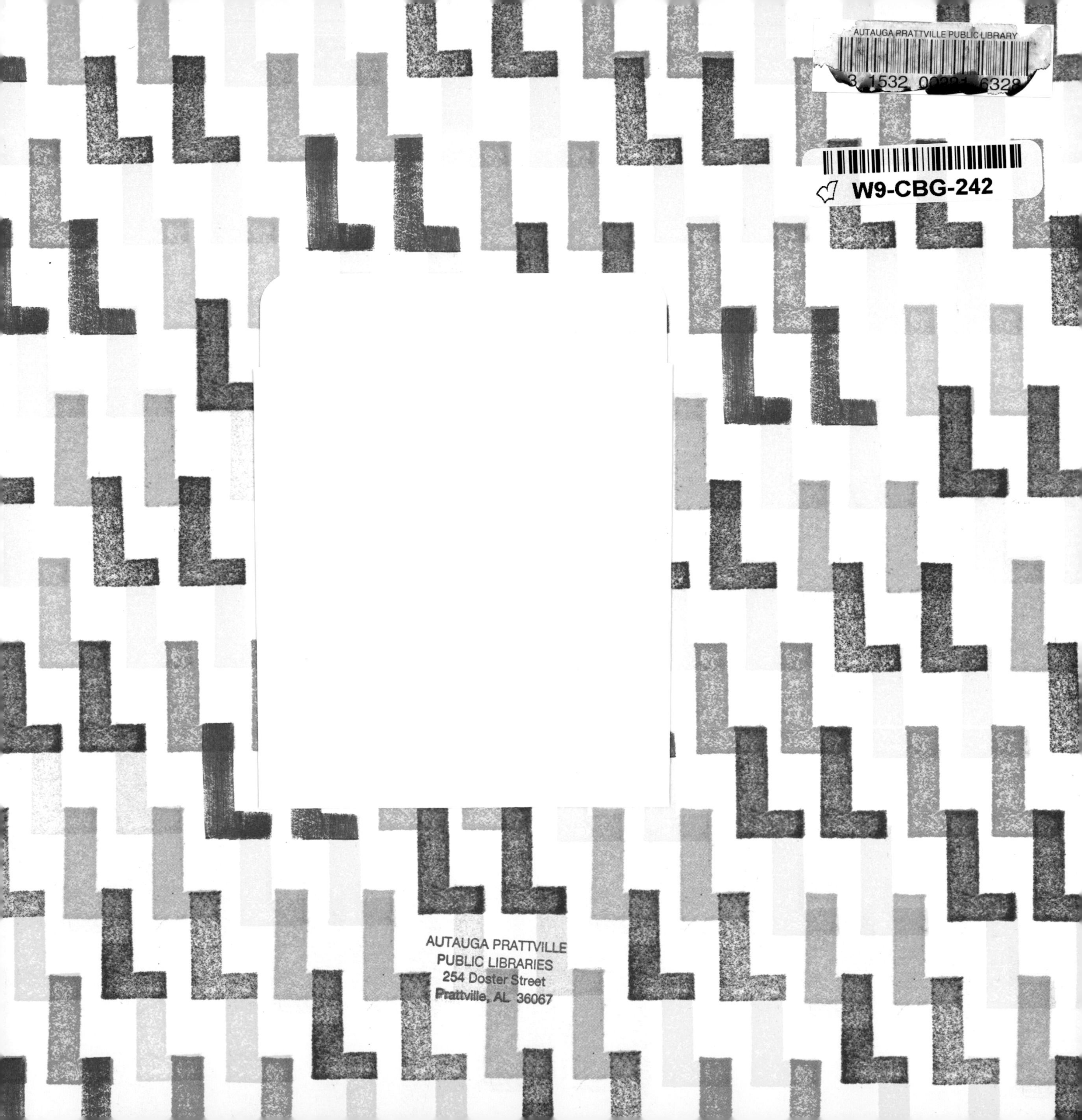

hello

yellow

For Denise

Hello

For information address HarperCollins Children's Books,
a division of HarperCollins Publishers, 195 Broadway, New York, NY 10007.
www.harpercollinschildrens.com

The artwork and hand-lettered text was created by hand-cut rubber stamps, stencils,
BLO pens, and additional pencil line work, all composited digitally.

Library of Congress Cataloging-in-Publication Data

Names: Woodcock, Fiona, author, illustrator.
Title: Hello / Fiona Woodcock.
Description: First edition. | New York, NY : Greenwillow Books, an imprint of HarperCollinsPublishers, [2019] |
Summary: "A brother and sister enjoy a brilliant day full of spills, thrills, and silly adventures
in this story comprised only of words that contain a double L"—Provided by publisher.
Identifiers: LCCN 2018045404 | ISBN 9780062644565 (trade ed.)
Subjects: | CYAC: Seashore—Fiction. | Play—Fiction. | Brothers and sisters—Fiction.
Classification: LCC PZ7.1.W656 Hel 2019 | DDC [E]—dc23
LC record available at https://lccn.loc.gov/2018045404

19 20 21 22 23 SCP 10 9 8 7 6 5 4 3 2 1
First Edition

Greenwillow Books
An Imprint of HarperCollins*Publishers*

FIONA WOODCOCK

valley

hilltop

BRILL

IANT

collide

YELL

9

a
op

HALL
of
Mirrors

TALL

small

ROLLERCOASTER

THRILL
SHRILL
(ILL)

hello

BEACH
BA

wallop
dollop

spi

chilly

silly

hello

jelly

fish

BILL

SHELLS

collect them ALL

CALL

follow

nightfall

marshmallow

COLLAPSE

ullaby

hello

pillo

W